MW00897161

Lexi and The Case of The Curious Red Cardinal

Story by Renee Rosenstein

Illustrations by Sam Roth

Editing & Book Formatting by
Elizabeth Klug, Word Watcher Editing

Dedicated to my wonderful grandsons,
Conrad and Kevin Goerl.

"What's that tapping at my window" said little Lexi. The little girl looked out and saw a red cardinal bird. He was hanging on the window and tapping his head against the screen. "Isn't that what a woodpecker does?" asked Lexi. Her grandmother remarked that the bird was just being curious.

The little red cardinal came back every day, and Lexi started to get very attached to him. "I think he wants to come into my room. I think I will adopt him and train him to do tricks." Her grandma replied, "He is a wild bird and cannot be tamed."

"Oh yes he can! I will train him. Just watch, Grandma, and you will see what happens." Her grandma smiled, enjoying her granddaughter's excitement.

The next day, Lexi heard the bird and quickly ran to the window. "Little bird, I am going to call you 'Ruby', just like the color of your feathers. I am going to give you treats." She slipped her finger through the two holes that the bird had made in the screen, and gave him a piece of a cracker.

Ruby ate it all up and banged his head against the screen. "You are welcome" said Lexi. The little bird never missed a day, and even in a rainstorm always appeared at the window.

One day, Lexi slipped her finger through the hole in the screen and Ruby jumped onto it. "Grandma, Grandma, come quickly. Ruby jumped on my finger." Her startled grandma proclaimed, "You must have magic fingers!"

The little bird came to the window every day. He got his snack, jumped on Lexi's finger and danced when she sang to him. Lexi was so happy that she trained her little red cardinal.

After a while, winter came and brought heavy snow. Weeks had passed and Lexi saw no sign of Ruby. "Oh Grandma, I don't think I'll ever see him again." Grandma replied, "Perhaps he went to a warmer place. Be patient my little one, and wait till the spring."

Spring finally came, and Lexi went to the window every single day, but saw no sign of Ruby. She was very sad.

Then one day she heard a tapping at the window screen. Lexi ran to find Ruby, who brought along his mate and two little baby birds. She put her finger through the screen, and he jumped on it. He took the treat and shared it with his new family. After one loud chirp, he flew away.

Lexi never saw Ruby again. Her grandma said, "He went to have a life with his family and wanted to say goodbye to you. You actually trained a wild bird. You are truly special and he will always remember you."

Lexi smiled because she knew Ruby would always be in her heart, and no one could ever take that memory away from her.

The End

ABOUT THE AUTHOR

Renee Rosenstein is a native New Yorker, born in the Bronx. She moved to Houston, Texas to be near her two grandsons. This is her first book, which was inspired by the stories she told her grandsons. Renee lives with her cat, Romeo, and is now working on her second book, with hopefully many more to come.

72357738R00018

Made in the USA
Middletown, DE
05 May 2018